Llamouth Valley

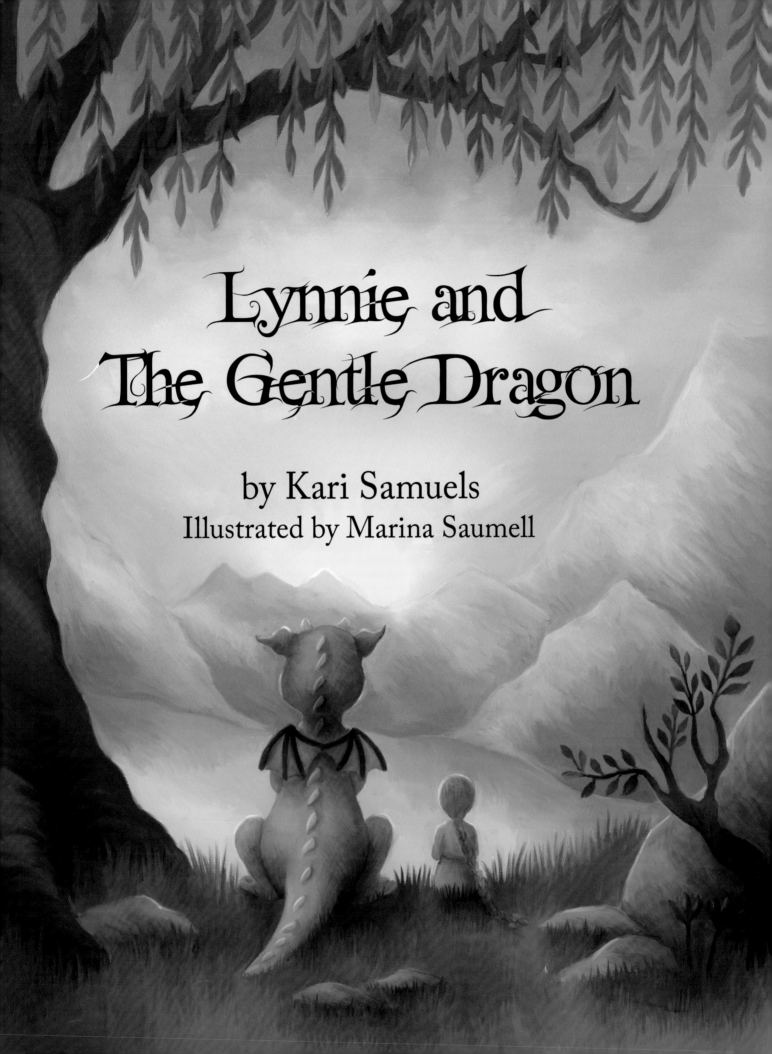

Lynnie and The Gentle Dragon

by Kari Samuels

Illustrated by Marina Saumell

First edition 2017
Published in the USA by Kari Samuels International, Inc.
Hardback ISBN: 978-0-9984880-2-8
Library of Congress Control Number: 2017901876

www.karisbooks.com

To my sweet nieces and nephews Michelle, Rachel, Daniel, Rebecca, Jacob, David, Maya, Emil and Liam. Never lose your wild side. May your life be filled with wondrous adventures, and you always have loving friends along your path.

In the valley called Llamouth, of heather and spice,
lives a gaggle of dragons.
They're all very nice.

Geldimere is known as the friendliest of all.
He warms chilly creatures,
both mighty and small.

One crisp autumn morning, just after night's freeze,
while gathering mushrooms, he heard a wee sneeze.

Shivering at his heels lay a sleeping young maid.
She had three feet of hair in a long golden braid.

Geldimere grew curious.
He sniffed at the floor,
for he had never seen a real human before.

The maiden awoke.
Geldimere smiled with glee.
He reached out his hand.
She ran up a tree.

He asked, "Hey, little person,
from whom do you hide?"
She cried, "Dragons have nostrils with fire inside!"

"Nay, nay," Geldimere chuckled.
"Those dragons are rare,
and handle their blazes with delicate care.

"Of all the dragons in Llamouth,
not one can be mean.
We come in infinite sizes
and great shades of green:

Earth Dragons.

Water Dragons,

Fairy Dragons too,

Even Musical Dragons
who play the kazoo!

Yet one thing is common, and this you will see;
our dragons are famous for hospitality.

"Come down from your willow! I'll care for that sneeze!
My friends call me Geldy. Your name, if you please?"

She said, "My name is Lynnie," while blowing her nose.
"I've been wandering so long my teeth nearly froze.

"Last night I was dreaming at home in my bed,
when along stole a witch with a wicked green head.
She tore me away on her wild witch's broom,
but she was so greedy she left me no room.

"As we rounded the moon, and flew down the bend,
I fell off the handle and bumped on my end.

"I've been roaming this valley in search of a way
to return to my homeland.
My school starts Monday!"

Geldimere pondered deeply.
He could not deny
a kind gesture to help her.
This was his reply:

"I would gladly escort you and not hesitate,
but my singular efforts would render us late.
I'm one trillion years old,
no little dawn more,
and don't earn my wings
'till I'm one trillion and four.
My father, however, is eight zillion and three,
and deep in his house hides a magic cup of tea.

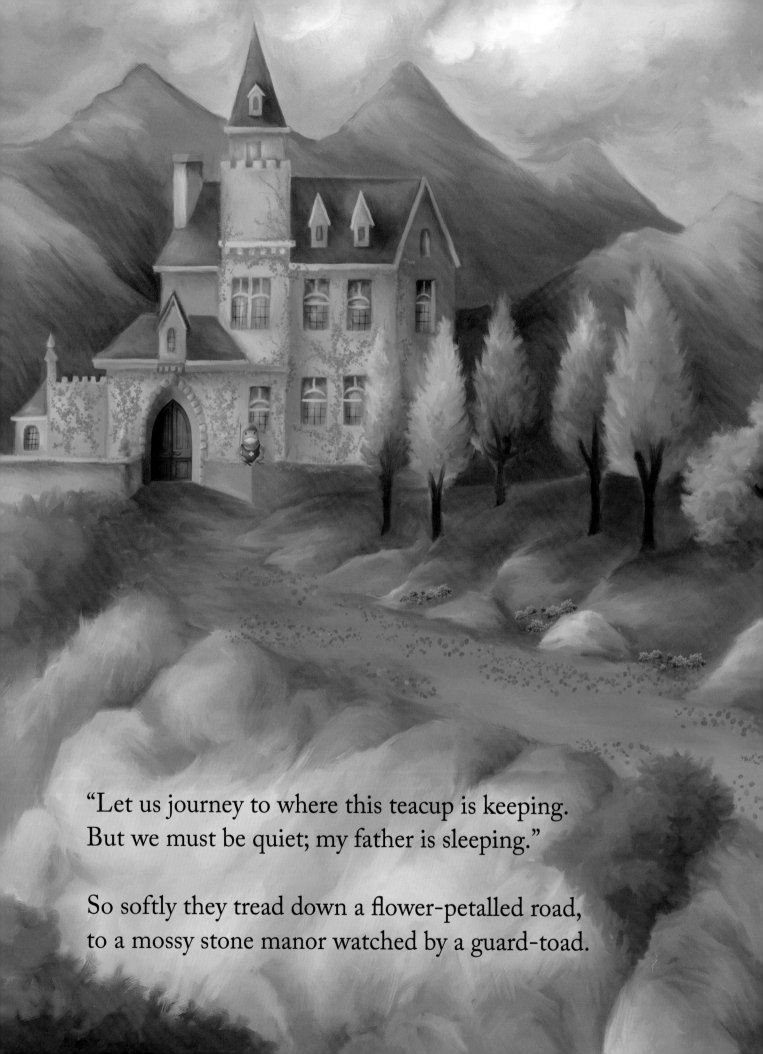

"Let us journey to where this teacup is keeping.
But we must be quiet; my father is sleeping."

So softly they tread down a flower-petalled road,
to a mossy stone manor watched by a guard-toad.

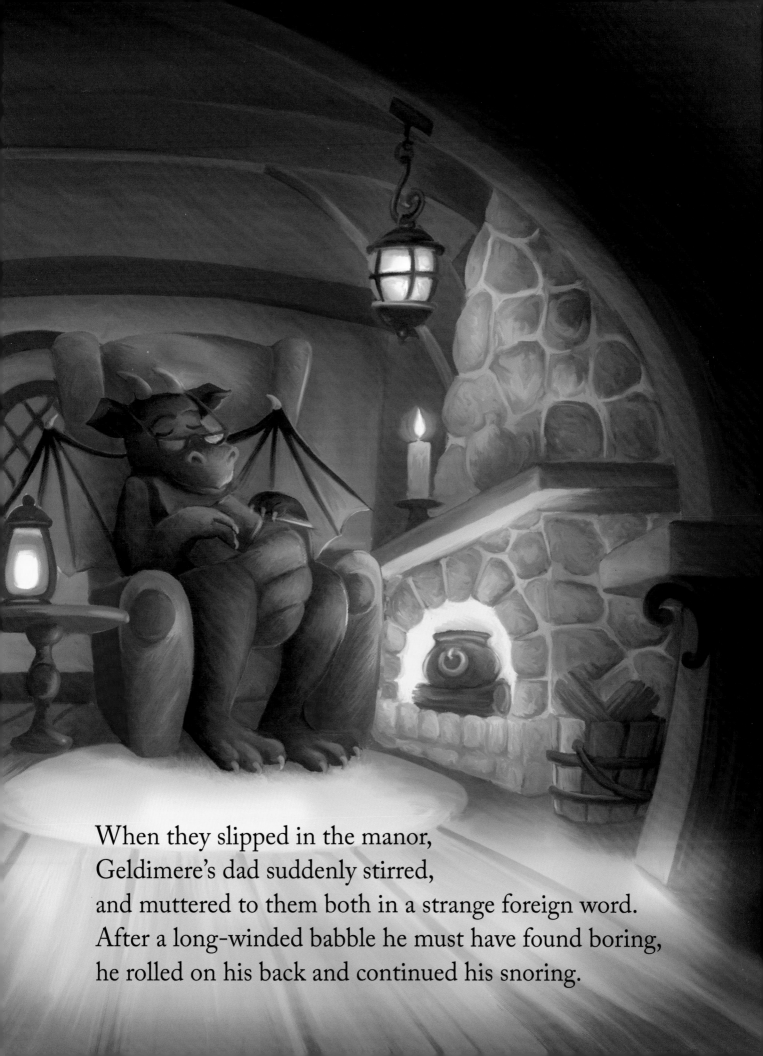

When they slipped in the manor,
Geldimere's dad suddenly stirred,
and muttered to them both in a strange foreign word.
After a long-winded babble he must have found boring,
he rolled on his back and continued his snoring.

Geldimere and Lynnie crept lightly through the house.

Lynnie muffled a squeal when she met with a mouse.

They tiptoed…
and scurried…

and tippy-toed some more.

At last! They reached the Enchanted Tea Room door.
Click! Click! The door swung open.
Then to Lynnie's surprise,
shone an emerald teacup, twenty times her size!

"Eureka!" Geldimere chimed.
"The teacup! Hop in!
Fasten your tea-belt!
Let's go for a spin!"

They flew…
    beyond the mountain treetops, over blue bubbling brooks,
      to a land with white crystals and soft moonlit nooks…

through a dazzling rainbow,
and a sky painted red…

until Lynnie was home warm and safe in her bed.

"Yippee!" Geldimere rejoiced.
Lynnie heaved a deep cry.
Geldimere wiped away her tears and said, "Tell me why!"

"I'll miss you, Sir Geldy, because I don't know when
I will ever be able to see you again."

Geldimere cupped her small hands in his wrinkled green palm.
He spoke softly in her ear.
She hushed to a calm.
He said:

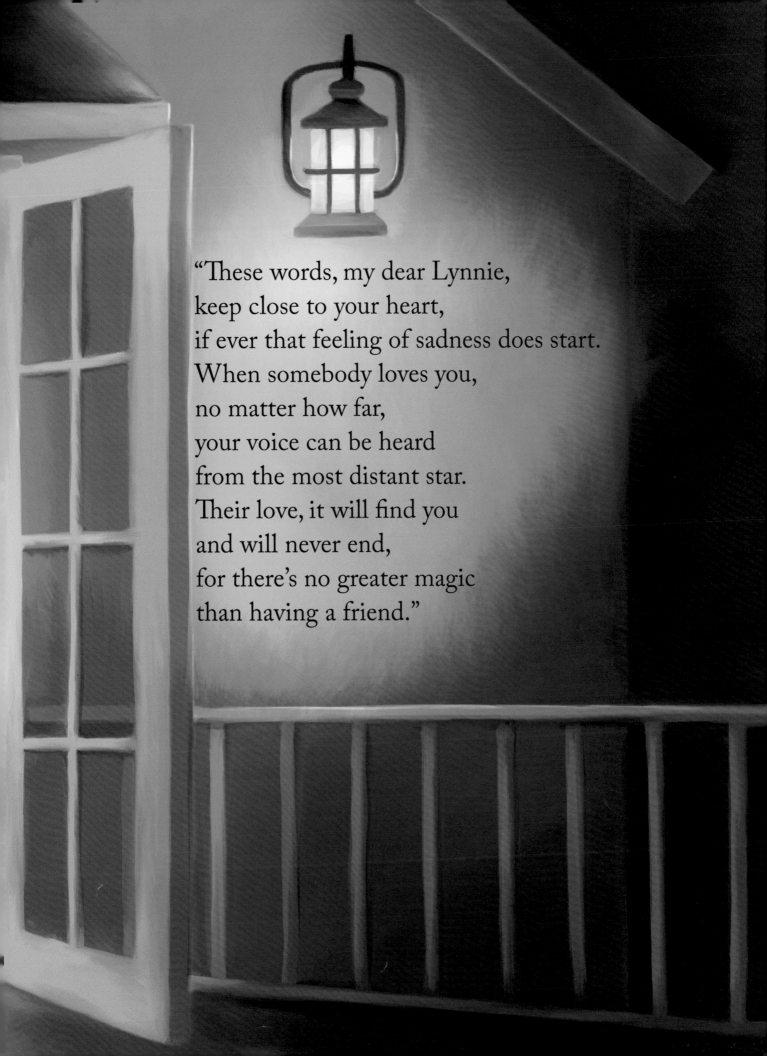

"These words, my dear Lynnie,
keep close to your heart,
if ever that feeling of sadness does start.
When somebody loves you,
no matter how far,
your voice can be heard
from the most distant star.
Their love, it will find you
and will never end,
for there's no greater magic
than having a friend."

Lynnie nestled these words like a snug little sheep.
Geldimere tucked her goodnight.
And she went
        quietly
            to sleep.

About the Author

Kari Samuels brings smiles to people all over the world as a Happiness Coach. Originally from New York City, she now gallivants around the globe with her wonderful husband Troy. She loves making furry, feathered, and human friends everywhere she goes.

When she's not dreaming about dragons, she can be found having an outdoor adventure, or dancing to her own rhythm. This is her first book.

Visit her at: karisbooks.com

About the Illustrator

Marina Saumell resides in Mar del Plata, Argentina with her husband and two children. She has a degree in Architecture and worked as an architect for several years. Her love for children's books inspired her to become a freelance illustrator following the birth of her first child.

She has brought dozens of delightful characters to life. She loves making magical worlds come alive through her colorful pages.

Join her at www.marimell.com

Printed in China

Friends Forever